FIREWORKS

PHOTOS + FACTS

027

A BRIGHTLY PHOTO-FACT BOOK

Copyright @ 2024, Brightly Books

All rights reserved. This book or any portion thereof may not be reproduced or used in any manner whatsoever without the express written permission of the copyright holder.

www.brightlybooks.com

Fireworks are amazing...

Fireworks are like big, sparkly art shows in the sky.

People use them to celebrate special days, like the Fourth of July.

There are many different kinds of fireworks.

Some go up in the air,
others stay on the ground.

Sparklers are handheld fireworks that sprinkle out sparks.

Fountains stay on the ground but shoot sparks high into the air.

Rockets shoot up into the sky before exploding into colors.

Some fireworks can make shapes with their sparkles! Can you see the hearts?

Firework makers use chemicals to create the bright colors.

Each type of firework has a special formula to make it unique.

To use a firework, an adult lights the fuse, which is like a long string.

The fuse burns and sets off
a small explosion.

This tiny explosion makes the firework shoot up into the air.

When it gets really high,
there is a big explosion!

With a loud boom and a crackle, the explosion lights up the sky!

Fireworks shows are big, bright, and noisy.

They happen at night so we can see all the colors shine.

A fireworks show starts slow, with a few fireworks, and then gets faster.

At the end of the show,
there is a big finale with
lots of fireworks all at once.

Boom! Crackle! The finale is the loudest part.

Fireworks can be a little
scary with their bright
colors and big sounds...

But they are awesome to see as they light up the night!

Fireworks are amazing!

Made in United States
Orlando, FL
07 December 2024